Dear Parents,

Reading—and enjoying the experience of having someone read to you—should be part of every child's life.

It is not only vital to education and literacy, it is an opening door to a wonderland of adventure and imagination. It is like experiencing another world right here on earth.

The Reading Buddies program from Reading Is Fundamental is a wonderful opportunity to take those first steps.

I am proud that Fievel has been selected to be the official Reading Buddies mascot. It may be the most important role he will ever play.

Steven Spielberg

We would like to give thanks to the following
contributors whose generosity helped make this
book possible:

AMBLIN ENTERTAINMENT
ARCATA GRAPHICS/HAWKINS
BEVERLY LAZOR-BAHR for her illustrations
MCA/UNIVERSAL

Library of Congress Cataloging-in-Publication Data
Herman, Gail, date. Fievel's big showdown / by Gail Herman : illustrated by Beverly Lazor-Bahr :
based on characters created by David Kirschner. p. cm. "Steven Spielberg presents An American
Tail." Summary: Fievel uses a clever trick to rescue his sister and their friends from a big cat, thus
proving he is not a fraidy mouse. ISBN 0-448-40379-X [1. Mice-Fiction. 2. Courage—Fiction.]
I. Lazor-Bahr, Beverly, ill. II. Kirschner, David, 1955– III. Title. PZ7.H4315Fi
1992 [E]—dc20 91-26285

A B C D E F G H I J

STEVEN SPIELBERG PRESENTS

An American Tail™

Fievel's Big Showdown

By Gail Herman
Illustrated by Beverly Lazor-Bahr
Based on characters created by David Kirschner

Grosset & Dunlap • New York

It is a sunny day
in Green River.
Fievel is reading a book.
The book is about a ghost
in a scary old house.
"Woo! Woo!" he reads.
"I am coming to get you."

All at once,

Fievel sees a shadow.

It is big.

It is scary.

"Help!" shouts Fievel.
"It is a ghost!"

"Silly!

It is only me,"

says his sister, Tanya.

"You are such a fraidy mouse."

"I am not,"
Fievel says.
"I was reading
a scary story."

"Read, read, read!"
says Tanya.
"Let's have a race.
Let's climb a tree.
Let's play in the
scary old house."
But Fievel does not want
to play now.
He wants to finish
his book.
Tanya does not understand.

"Fievel is a fraidy mouse!"
Tanya tells the other mice.

"We are not fraidy mice,"
they shout.
And everybody runs off
to the scary old house.

Everybody but Fievel.

He reads and reads.

There!

He is done.

What a good book!

Fievel looks around.

It is late now.

But where is Tanya?

"I will find her," he says.

Fievel goes to

the scary old house.

It <u>is</u> scary.

It <u>is</u> old.

Just like the house

in the story!

But Fievel goes in anyway.

Inside, it is dark.

Fievel goes up the stairs.

Creak.

Fievel opens a door.

Creak.

There is Tanya!

The mice are in trouble!

19

"Cat R. Waul is here!"
Tanya tells Fievel.
"He is going to turn us
into mouseburgers!"

Fievel sees the bad cat.

He looks hungry.

Fievel must save his friends.

But how?

Cat R. Waul is a big cat.

Fievel is a little mouse.

Then Fievel remembers.

Tanya is a little mouse, too.

But her shadow was big.

Fievel also remembers

his book about the ghost.

Fievel has a plan.

"It is time for a showdown!"

he says.

First Fievel sets the mice free.

Then he gets a napkin.

Fievel puts the napkin
over his head.

He steps in front of a light.

Fievel waves his arms.

"Woo! Woo!

I am coming to get you!"

calls Fievel.

"Leave the mice alone.

Leave the mice

a-l-o-o-o-n-e."

Cat R. Waul sees the shadow—
the BIG shadow.

"Yowl!" Cat R. Waul shouts.

"A ghost!"

He runs out of the house.

No mouseburgers for him.

The mice are saved!

"Hooray!

Hooray for Fievel!"

"You are not a fraidy mouse,"
Tanya says.

"You just like to read."

"And I am glad you do!"